Barbie Fairytopia
MERMAIDIA

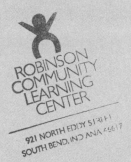

By Mary Man-Kong • Based on the original screenplay by Elise Allen
Cover photography by the Mattel Photo Studio

Special thanks to Rob Hudnut, Tiffany J. Shuttleworth, Vicki Jaeger, Monica Okazaki,
Mainframe Entertainment, Luke Carroll, Mike Douglas, Dave Gagnon, Derek Goodfellow, Teresa Johnston,
Anita Lee, Sean Newton, Kelly Shin, Julia Ferguson, Byron Leboe, and Walter P. Martishius

A Random House PICTUREBACK® Book
Random House 🏠 New York

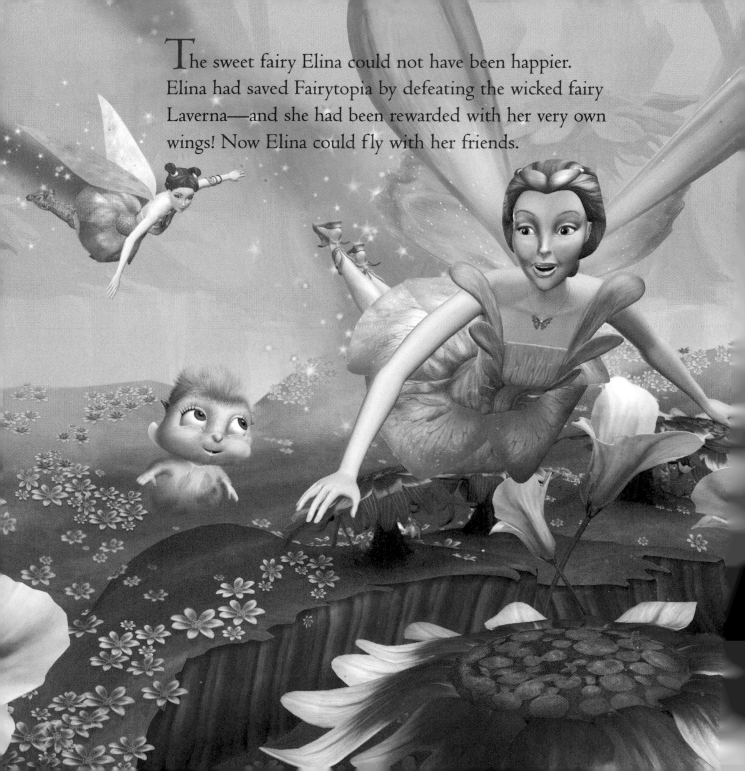

The sweet fairy Elina could not have been happier.
Elina had saved Fairytopia by defeating the wicked fairy
Laverna—and she had been rewarded with her very own
wings! Now Elina could fly with her friends.

Laverna, however, was furious! A spell had been cast on the evil fairy, trapping her in the Bogs of the Hinterland. The only way Laverna could break the spell was to eat the magical Immunity Berry. But only the royal Mermaidia family knew where it was hidden. So Laverna commanded her henchmen, the Fungi, to kidnap Mermaidia's Prince Nalu.

Luckily, Prince Nalu saw the Fungi approaching. Before he was captured, he sent a sea butterfly to ask Elina for help. Elina, her puffball, Bibble, and the sea butterfly raced to the Crystal Cove to rescue the prince.

A beautiful mermaid named Nori blamed Elina for the prince's disappearance. "Every time you're around, there's trouble," Nori said to Elina. "Last time, the Firebirds invaded the Crystal Cove, and now the Fungi have kidnapped Prince Nalu."

Nori dove into the water and swam away. Elina tried to follow, but she couldn't breathe underwater. Luckily, an adorable turtle named Tutu and a playful dolphin named Fin-Fin offered her some magic seaweed. Elina and Bibble nibbled the seaweed, and suddenly, they could breathe just like fish! They followed Tutu and Fin-Fin down to the enchanted world of Mermaidia.

Elina soon found Nori and tried to reason with her.
"We need to work together to find Prince Nalu," Elina
said. "We can't do it by ourselves."

Nori finally agreed to help her.

Together, Elina and Nori sought the advice of the
Merfairies. The tiny fairies told them where to find
Delphine, the oracle, who could help with their quest.

Elina and Nori traveled to the edge of Mermaidia to see Delphine, a wise old snail.

"To find Prince Nalu, you will need great underwater strength," Delphine warned Elina. "You must trade your wings for a mermaid's tail. Then you'll be able to swim through the Depths of Despair and find the Mirror of the Mist."

"But I can't give up my wings," Elina cried. "I'm a fairy."

The snail gave Elina a beautiful blue pearl necklace. "If you need to, you can use these pearls to wish for a tail," Delphine said. "If you are out of the water before the last pearl turns white, you will get your wings back. If not, you will remain a mermaid forever."

Elina and Nori thanked Delphine, then swam into the Depths of Despair. Suddenly, long strands of seaweed wrapped around Nori. She was trapped!

Elina remembered the pearls that Delphine had given her. "Please let me save my friend," Elina wished. Magically, Elina's wings disappeared and her legs transformed into a beautiful mermaid's tail! Elina quickly swam down to Nori and untangled her from the seaweed.

"Thank you, Elina," Nori said gratefully. "I can't believe it—you're a mermaid!"

Elina and Nori hurried toward an enormous clamshell. A friendly fish swam out and showed them a mirror—it was the Mirror of the Mist! In the mirror, they saw Prince Nalu held captive in the Fungi's hideaway. The fish blew a magical bubble that would lead them there.

As they followed the bubble, Elina, Nori, and Bibble passed a cave filled with berries.

"If you eat one of those berries, it will reveal your true self," Nori explained.

Elina eyed the beautiful berries and then picked one. She had a plan.

The three friends raced to the Fungi's hideaway. There they secretly switched the Immunity Berry with the true-self berry.

As the Fungi escaped with the true-self berry, they dropped a bottle of poison into Mermaidia's waters. Elina bravely dove after it. At that very instant, the last blue pearl in her necklace turned white—and in a fantastic flash of light, Elina became a mermaid forever!

The Fungi rushed back to the Bogs of the Hinterland and gave Laverna the berry. Thinking it was the Immunity Berry, the evil fairy ate it and was transformed. The true-self berry had turned her into a toad!

"*Aaaah!*" wailed Laverna. "I'll get you, Elina!"

Elina was glad that all the merpeople were safe. But she was also sad that she had lost her wings.

"You're the same person, no matter how you look," Nori said. "And if you eat this true-self berry, it should reveal your true self."

Elina nibbled the berry. Suddenly, her mermaid tail vanished and the most magnificent wings appeared!

"I'm so happy!" Elina exclaimed. "I'm a fairy again!"